I0694197

HEAVIER THAN A DEATH IN THE FAMILY

Craig Dyer was born in the town of Blackpool, in the North West of England, and now lives in Berlin. With his musical project, *The Underground Youth*, he has toured around the world and released ten albums since 2008. In 2019 a collection of Craig's lyrics and poetry was released under the title *The Devil In Me & In All The Rest*. This was followed in 2021 by *Into The Aether*, a book of short stories.

Heavier Than A Death In The Family is his latest book, released by Far West Press.

This book is dedicated to the members of my own band, especially my wife Olya, for without whom neither the band, nor this book, would exist.

In memory of Takashi Mizutani

Written
in
Berlin
Warsaw
&
Prague
2021

Part I

Mae

A day off in Florence. She opens her lips ever so slightly and runs the scarlet lipstick across the soft skin that forms the edge of her mouth. After she has hauled herself up onto the base of the statue, she swings her slender arms around his magnificently built, muscular neck. She looks down at me and winks before planting a lipstick kiss onto the face of the marble sculpture, leaving behind her bright red trace on the five hundred year old cheek. Ah Isa, my love.

It's not the alarm that wakes you, no. It's a phone call, beauty being intruded upon, internal cursing, flashbacks to being on tour, unwelcome hotel room wakeups. But, I'm at home and my phone is vibrating deep into the pillow beside me.

'This better be good…'

'You've not seen the news?'

'What news?' An involuntary yawn follows.

'*The* news.' I blindly reach across the mattress, find cold aluminium, I pull the laptop up beside me, open, login. 'Hang on.' I exhale into the phone speaker and drop it down beside me so that I can type in and load the Great British News home page. The website stutters for a few seconds, as if weighed upon by an unfamiliar gravity, and then it appears, Holden's face, my best friend and in spite of the uncertainty of the past month, the singer in my band.

The Night Collectors

Formed in Manchester by guitarist and songwriter Mae Mulligan, bassist Francis Bhatt, drummer Johnny Byrne and singer Holden, The Night Collectors take their name from a song by Japanese noise rock band, Les Rallizes Dénudés. The Collectors' own unique brand of noise rock has hit a wider audience than the genre would typically allow, gaining them a worldwide cult fanbase over the seven years they have been together and the four albums they have released. Prior to the controversial restrictions placed on British musicians, The Night Collectors completed tours of Europe, Asia and the Americas to underground acclaim. As a band they have also been at the forefront of protesting the British government's prohibitions against musicians and the excessive regulation and banning of overseas performances. They are soon to embark on an extensive tour of the UK.

September

Thursday 2nd - Durham
Friday 3rd - Newcastle
Saturday 4th - Edinburgh
Sunday 5th - Aberdeen
Monday 6th - Day Off
Tuesday 7th - Glasgow
Wednesday 8th - Carlisle
Thursday 9th - Lancaster
Friday 10th - Liverpool
Saturday 11th - Manchester
Sunday 12th - Day Off

Monday 13th - Leeds
Tuesday 14th - Hull
Wednesday 15th - Sheffield
Thursday 16th - Stoke-on-Trent
Friday 17th - Birmingham
Saturday 18th - Cardiff
Sunday 19th - Bristol
Monday 20th - Day Off
Tuesday 21st - Rugby
Wednesday 22nd - Northampton
Thursday 23rd - Norwich
Friday 24th - London
Saturday 25th - Brighton
Sunday 26th - Day Off
Monday 27th - Portsmouth
Tuesday 28th - Southampton
Wednesday 29th - Plymouth
Thursday 30th - Leicester

October

Friday 1st - Nottingham
Saturday 2nd - Manchester

Holden

A silent scream reverberates around your skull.

It's not the alarm that wakes you, no. Certainly not any fervent desire to open your eyes. It feels like someone's rammed a wire brush down my throat. A cough. An indistinct taste of stale cigarettes and blood. *So* dehydrated. The torturous desire to drink water with a bladder so full to bursting that it hurts to move. It's something of a combination of all these things that prevents me from rolling over and falling back to sleep, and considering Mae sounds like she's having a shower a mere arms length away from my head, I'd wager I have between ten and fifteen minutes to be down at the van. It aches to stand, that interminable early morning back pain, I never would have thought that by my early thirties I'd have reached an age at which it hurts to wake up. A few new knocks to the legs too, from on stage? In the crowd? From loading out the gear? In the bar afterwards? Yesterday? The day before? I can't fight the urge to piss anymore, if Mae's locked the bathroom door then it's going out the window. I try the handle, she screams at me to get out but I'm already holding it in my hand and the process is underway. I apologise and she curses me from the shower, the warm moist steam engulfs me as the relief of emptying my bladder feels almost as good as any high I've had in the past days. I make the motion as if to shield my eyes and turn to ask Mae how long we have. Less than fifteen minutes. Back in the room I gather the pile of clothes from beside my bed and dress, drink down the bottle of water I left on the nightstand and what remains in the bottle of wine I left by the phone. I call down to reception to ask what time breakfast is served until. We've missed it. I smoke a cigarette out of the window and wait for Mae to dress and pack her bag so we can head down to meet the others at the van. I don't know where we're heading today but I hope it's a long enough drive for me to get some more sleep.

Mae

We've only been on tour for one week and the van is already a veritable slum on wheels. Bits of indefinable matter exist in any crevice that can't be cleaned by brushing your hand across it. Sticky patches of stale spilt beer and wine, the public house aroma mixed with that of heavy sweat and unwashed body odour. There's an overwhelming intensity to living in such close quarters in such self-imposed squalor, it doesn't *need* to be approached in such a manner, but as a band this has always been our way, and somehow it works in bringing us closer together. When any other combination of people would be driven apart by such circumstances, we formed a bond akin to that of a gang, no, we're more like a family.

Anyway, I locate and throw out the stinking bin liner, that's something. An ebb tide flowing to the distant sea. The flood always returns in time. Holden climbs into his corner and closes his eyes behind the sunglass shade, Francis hands me a coffee and tells me how the mediocre breakfast was worth missing for that extra time in bed. Ronnie, our driver, is behind the wheel and I'm told Johnny was locked in the bathroom when Francis came down, we're always waiting for one. Every now and then, it's me.

Johnny

The distances you cover when touring the UK are child's play. Rarely more than a couple of hours on the road, depending on routing. Sometimes that's fucked up by how the tour's been booked. Zigzagging backwards forwards back and past again. When we used to drive ourselves we'd miss a turning or fuck up the directions, Manchester to London once took us eight hours. Fortunately those days are long behind us now that we have Ronnie. Anyway, compared to Eastern Europe or the States, it's nothing.

I can't sleep in the van so I welcome the shorter drive. When it's long though, or through the night, I just sit in silence and absorb my surroundings while the others sleep. Sometimes I'll sit with Ronnie in the front to keep her company while she drives through the darkness, but we all know well that she prefers her solitude, so it can be a little awkward.

In the back, propped up in my seat, head resting on a pillow I lifted from one of the nicer hotels - always one of the chain brands, never a boutique or family run place - the street lights reflect off all the elements and surfaces within the van, detailing momentarily in fleeting bars of light through the darkness, what exists within our roving camp. Illuminating the faces of my band mates, distorted in light and shadow like they're putting on a private freak show for me and my eyes alone. Their expressions appear to change, the naked structure, intention laid bare. Their inner feelings, thoughts and dreams. Do my own betray the same? I ask questions of myself to assist in the passing of time. I get embroiled in internal monologues and futile disputes of the self. It's not surprising really, the exhaustion takes its toll and has its filthy rotten way with you. Promoters and fans don't always realise what you put yourself through, that every day, but for a few minor changes, is essentially the same. They experience just one evening with you, a fraction of the reality in which we find ourselves living. And in honesty it's no way to live. Waking early, tired, hungover, drunk, when on time you eat breakfast, but usually you're not so you get in the van, drive, read, talk, think, listen, drink, arrive at the venue, load-in, eat some welcoming food - you have to put that inside of you whether you like it or not - another drink, set up the stage, soundcheck, then you're waiting around - that's really got to be about eighty-five percent of this job, waiting around - another drink, you start to feel a little better, maybe you go check in to the hotel, lie down momentarily, shower occasionally, back to the venue, you put some more food inside of you, it goes down easier now, the drink is levelling you out, then you wait around some more, maybe you watch the support band, maybe you don't, the pre-stage ritual - set up, setlists, stage drinks - then you play - the reason we put up with all the rest - but before you know it you're finished, encore, it's over, you drink, socialise, sign a record, shake hands, stand for a photo, maybe there's someone to talk to, a girl who's interested, whoever, you drink more, pack down the equipment, load the van, get paid, make a plan for the next morning, go to a bar, drink more, snort a line, maybe swallow a pill, drink, back to the hotel, maybe you brought someone with you, in that case sex - when you still can - and pass out, wake up and do it all over again. Repetition, repetition, repetition. It's fucking psychotic. And unlike the others, I can't sleep in the damn van.

Holden

Johnny, I've known for a decade or more now.

He's a gifted painter, his slender Irish drummers hands summon these stunning abstract oil works, sometimes slightly erotic, sometimes not. One of my favourites - he said he'd give me but never did - depicts a man and a woman bound to each other by chains, one extending from their hearts and the other from their genitals. I'm not saying it's steeped in complex allegory or anything, I just really love that painting. It fills me with an intense aesthetic pleasure, something in the brushstrokes or the colour. As a man Johnny's deeply flawed, as are we all. But above all else he's a character of immense strength and support. He's like a brother, sometimes older, sometimes younger, but always present. And always handsome. To say of him he held an androgynous beauty would not be untrue, but his features were neither masculine nor feminine, paradoxically they were at once both hard and delicate. I'd never tell him any of this though, we'd never hear the end of it.

Francis

Sometimes when you're performing on stage you're totally absorbed in that world, the dream you simply refuse to wake from. The ideal mixture of sound and light, each triggering a different sensory experience. Synaesthesia. Then at a hiss the smoke machine engulfs you in enough fog that you don't need to focus on the crowd, the venue, even the rest of the band. It's a solo experience. When that's *not* the case, however, you look out at the faces that are looking at you. You focus on those that catch your eye, that stunningly attractive girl in the front row who just won't stop making eye contact. But then I find myself thinking, *her skin is beautiful, but one day she'll turn from bronze to green, like an old penny, underground and nailed within a box*. And I'm like - What the fuck, where did that come from? These are the kind of bizarre thoughts that enter my mind when my hands are working through muscle memory and my brain is free to wander.

But shit, since the regulations came into place, that seems to be all that I can think about on stage. See, the government slowly imposed these artistic restrictions that amongst other things prevent British musicians from touring outside of the UK. I mean, that used to be one of the best things about this job, travelling, meeting people and immersing yourself in a different culture every couple of days. But the problem is that they can't *control* that, and beyond all else what this current government desires is unparalleled control. Or the idea of such a thing. They've silenced and drowned out the voices of others too, an all censoring wave of suppression. Journalists, writers, poets, artists, models, actors, sports personalities. You think, how far does it need to go? Who's next? The barman at your local pub? No, it's no joke. We seriously contemplated stopping playing altogether, but then these protest concerts started popping up and a few bands travelled to Europe and the States to play *illegally*. The first few to get caught just got stuck at the border with release fines to pay and additionally having to agree to *open surveillance* upon themselves and their families, but we also heard stories about others being detained indefinitely and there's rumours that some have gone *missing* on their return to the UK. You know, we're not talking exclusively about suspected terrorists or revolutionary dissidents here, we're talking about a twenty something year old musician who wants to go to France to play a punk rock concert in the sweaty basement of a bar. It's gone beyond nonsensical.

Anyway, here we are on this UK tour that our agent had to work tirelessly to arrange, in this current climate, it's just getting harder. And believe me, those in charge aren't fond of us playing here at home either. If they can put a stop to that, believe me, they will. And that's probably more a case of not *if*, but *when*. For now our shows are attended by undercover officers surveilling what we say and do on stage. And you don't need to be told who they are, how blatantly they stand out they might as well be wearing their fucking uniforms.

Mae

Francis was the last member to join the band, Johnny, Holden and myself had been looking for a competent bass player for a while and then a friend introduced us. Half Indian, half Scottish, heavy drinking, builds guitar pedals, loves noise, hates inequality, available for any rehearsal, any show, any time, any place. He didn't just learn all the songs we had in less than twenty-four hours, he lumbered into the rehearsal space to the jingle jangle of the chains around his cowboy boots, carrying this shattered old guitar case, having written brand new arrangements that transformed what we were trying to achieve with The Night Collectors. He made the band a band, and looked better than the rest of us whilst doing so. He can play the fool, but does so in knowing there can be a beauty to foolishness, a collapse of sense leading to an outcome that no reason could have predicted. That's Francis, the self-proclaimed *dark talisman* of the group.

We've arrived in Leeds earlier than anyone should ever arrive in Leeds. Fortunately the hotel rooms were ready and we didn't have to wait around to check in. Holden didn't sleep and is still clinging on to last night's inebriation, so we're at least fortunate enough that he might get a couple of hours before soundcheck. Otherwise it's only with great wild effort that I can contain my contempt for how he acts in that condition.

I fall face first into the pillow, unsuccessfully attempting to wring the fatigue out from every cell of my body. It will take more than a mere moment of motionlessness to achieve anything close to rejuvenation. I turn and prop myself up in bed with the pillow, looking across at Holden, completely passed out across his mattress in the most bizarre of angles. He sort of pulses imperceptibly with the motions of his internal blood flow, a heartbeat pumping intoxicated blood to every corner of his body. He's soundless, however, unnervingly so. Do I cross the room to check his breathing? I watch him for a short while before sinking my head down into the pillow and closing my eyes.

On tour I miss certain home comforts, like cooking my own food rather than wondering on a daily basis if we'll be dining in a fine restaurant or scraping some unidentifiable rice dish out of a microwaveable plastic bag. Deciding when, if at all, I will leave the house that day. Oh and waking up without that split second panic, anxiety and confusion over what bed in what room in what city in what country I am. I try to ensure that the last thought that fogs my mind, before I inevitably pass out, is a fond one.

I think about Isa and the way her face changes when she talks about the things she loves. I noticed this trait from the very beginning, so when I heard her mention my name during a phone conversation just prior to us leaving Italy and I saw that curl of her lip and slight crease beneath her nostrils, I knew before she said it to my face, through tears at the airport gate, that she loved me.

Johnny

You know, Holden has a sharp sarcastic side that at times can impress people as extremely arrogant, but he is in truth a soft and fair-minded person. Or at least I can say I've surmised as much from our, what must it be now? *Ten* years of friendship. We're talking here about a narcissistic man, let there be no mistaking it. But for all faults, I consider Holden a brother. He's an idealistic man, one that thinks everything can be very easily solved, even the most complex of world issues. It drives me crazy sometimes but I must respect his optimism, no, *optimism* isn't the word, it's more of a confidence. As if his own self-confidence should, in his mind, transmit to any and every situation that exists in the world. Honestly though, he was the reason we pushed so hard against the restrictions and joined the movement in playing those protest concerts. That was *all* Holden. At the time I accused him of doing it out of some self-serving righteousness to feed his own fame and ego. Yeah, he got pretty pissed about that. Hmm, rightly so. His discontented expression assumed an odd glow as rage brewed internally.

'To insinuate that I consider my own fame at all is the worst insult you've ever thrown at me!' I'd have anticipated that look that comes across his face in which you can see he's playing through in his mind clocking you in the jaw, but what I got was worse, he looked like he wanted to fucking disown me. I apologised later. In hindsight I couldn't be happier that he forced us to push onwards and upwards and against, and I'm so fucking glad that we did.

Holden

The Prime Minister, Sir Roger Lawrence. Sure, I've heard the line, *don't trust anyone who calls himself an ordinary man*. But fuck me, you certainly shouldn't take the word of a politician who has in all seriousness referred to himself as *extraordinary*. I read of the profound danger of leaders - *Invariably the most dangerous people seek the power*. Without name dropping history's most obvious tyrants, not many have sought it out quite like Lawrence. He had an almost messianic air of shiftiness and duplicity, the people's conman. Neat hair cleverly combed to conceal a receding hairline. A clean shiny face of uncompromising severity, a wide grin and eyes like long collapsed stars.

His government, this government, this immutable regime, has been in place for almost six years now. As a band we've existed for just one more than that. They remain unopposed by any mainstream alternative and unforgiving in quashing the rise of any unconventional opposition. The effete resistance initially took to the streets, they whispered *revolution* from behind their masks and then scuttled off into the shadows in fear of the consequences. All the while, and over the years, Lawrence has tightened his ruling royal white glove around the throat that used to speak of equality and fairness and acceptance. Preying on a nation's distrust, polarisation and frustration, fuelled by Lawrence's empty rhetoric and now reduced to fear and control by the terrifying surveillance of what must surely be considered at this point, a police state. A piranha-like paranoia that nibbled away until there was nothing left. No sense or rationale, just a country's national malaise.

The pulse of my blood burns and itches with each heavily censored or controlled news story that I read celebrating the latest stifling law that in some way transpires to infringe on our freedom whilst managing to be *for our own good*. Forget freedom of the press, salute farewell to ethics and standards. Welcome the retrogression to subservience, the likes of which this country will never have seen before. We currently stand on a slowly forming foundation of terror. A balancing act of risk versus survival. Head down, keep calm, carry on. That's it old boy.

What cultural differences exist, exist despite everything. I talk now not of liberty, human rights and civic responsibility - which we're currently witnessing the disintegration of within our own country - but the minor societal differences in social behaviours and customs. People are divided by the simplest, most basic emotions and understandings. You can share and have everything in common with another person, but nothing divides you more than that difference in culture. As a musician on the road, certainly at our level, you experience and appreciate that above all else. To strip us of that isn't to strip us of some diplomatic reasoning between countries, but it strips the individuals involved from not just broadening their horizons, but bringing the horizon so close that you feel as though you can enter it. The gift of transforming yourself and adapting to a different world that suits you better. When the freedom to travel opens these doors, you walk through them. When the door is locked, you don't even think to ask for the key. And I'm not concerned for us, but for those growing up in this environment who will never know what that felt like. Their horizon remains in a literal state of being so far beyond their grasp that it's also beyond their imagination. When that remains the case, only a small handful of these young people will reach out towards it, what a tragic state of affairs.

Francis

My clothes are filthy, the sweat from performing night after night dries into my jeans and the decaying leather of my jacket's armpits. I'm sitting in the van working on a warm can of lager that hopefully between him and his two brothers in the crate, can medicate my hazy head. It's like an unknown expedition touring through the Midlands, you never know what to expect. It might be a packed, pissed up crowd having the night of their lives, or it might be three or four pub locals hocking up phlegm in the silence between songs. Last night was something else though, it felt like the crowd was starving, scratching around on the floor for a morsel of matter to ingest. We played tight, proficient and really fucking loud. You can tell when the rest of the band are enjoying it as much as you are, if I look back at Johnny and his head is up taking it in, rather than down between his shoulders like he's praying to his long lost belief, if Mae's swinging her guitar around rather than motionlessly shoegazing, and if Holden is rolling around on the floor or deep within the crowd, I know it's more than just an alcohol buzz making me think it's a good show. It just feels *right*.

But here, now, in the back of the van, there are snores ringing out from Mae and Holden and Johnny's face is tucked in a Faulkner novel. I reach across and slip the book from Mae's lap, early existentialism from the Danish mind. Kierkegaard. *For dying means that it is all over, but dying the death means to live to experience death; and if for a single instant this experience is possible, it is tantamount to experiencing it forever.* The sickness unto death? No kidding. Can we lighten this darkness somehow? Jesus fucking Christ I'm sat in a van with a headache these beers just won't shift, stuck in traffic between Stoke-on-Trent and Birmingham, life is bleak enough.

Johnny

The days swim by, both completely unique and yet

somehow filled with the exact same routine. A heady and intoxicated haze of different faces and bodies in different rooms and spaces, but repeating the same actions, performing the same songs, reliving the same conversations. It begins to blur so that what happened yesterday or the day before feels more dreamlike than anything your sleeping mind can conjure. You question what actually happened against what you quite conceivably could have just imagined. On climbing into the back of the van in the morning we regale our individual stories from the previous evening. Mae, or more often than not Francis, will tell me I almost started a fight, or that I could have easily picked up this girl or even that guy if I hadn't been too inebriated to talk. Maybe I jumped over a bar and started serving my own drinks, started a rousing rendition of an Irish folk song that had a crowd chanting my name, or maybe I ended up thrown out into an alleyway like a sack of trash. Whether I went to bed with a goddess or woke up covered in my own vomit, it matters not. See, whether you're feeling pride or shame, the tour moves on, the van, life, time, evidently unstoppable, like a river or a stream, carrying you along, whether you feel the urge to pause for a moment or not.

Mae

I watch Holden as he caresses the edges of the empty glass that had held his whiskey or rum or whatever poison it had been. In an almost trance-like state he studies it deeply as if mourning the drinks passing. I can hear through the wall of our tiny backstage the quick death of the feedback the support band had left droning at the end of their set, and had now swiftly returned on stage to kill. That gives us around fifteen or twenty minutes until we play. I give Holden a sharp kick in the shin with the pointed tip of my boot, his eyes blink, open wide and his head snaps up. The room is aggressively lit by the denuded yellow light of the fluorescent tubes that hang above us. I watch his eyes adjust.

'We're on in fifteen.' In recognition of my words he silently nods and glances blankly around as if awakening from a decade long coma. 'You alright?' I ask.

'Oh, I'm fine, how long... How long were they playing for?' As Holden asks he reaches over to the table between us and fills his glass with a fistful of ice from the bucket and then unscrews a bottle of sparkling water and pours it over the top.

'I'm not sure, thirty minutes, maybe forty.' He knocks back the glass of water and returns it to the table to cover the ice cubes with a heavy measure from a bottle of scotch.

'It felt like a fucking lifetime.' He smirks and hands me the bottle before pushing a clean glass across to my side of the table. I return a smile and fill my own glass with the ice and cheap whiskey, lift and connect the two drinks in the air so the still smoky atmosphere of the room is briefly filled with a sharp crystal ring.

'To the lifetimes spent waiting.'

We've worked harder than anyone understands to get to this point. In this industry, for a band such as ours, it's an incessant crusade. A constant campaign of self-promotion, touring, writing, recording, releasing, promoting and keeping the wheels greased and turning. Progress is not linear. It's a vortex of chance and luck and if the fanbase that keeps you afloat were to forget about you, you'd be twisted up and torn apart. We're thankful to them, our cult following, without whom we'd have long since had to have given up, we'd each be working in an office or on a phone or in a kitchen or behind a bar. I haven't the first idea what Holden would be doing. Nor myself for that matter. But whatever, wherever, there's not a chance anything could replace what we currently consider ourselves lucky to do for a living.

Holden

Being in the Midlands I have the opportunity to drop in on an old, albeit untrustworthy friend. I visit him for pills primarily, Oxycodone, Codeine, Zolpidem, Benzodiazepines, some of the best I can acquire without any questions being raised other than those so utterly ridiculous that they catch you quite unaware -

'You have any interest in firearms?' If you can imagine this being said in a Black Country accent, then please do.

'No. Wait, you sell guns now?'

'Just on the side y'know, drugs are still my main peddle.' An awkward moment of silence follows as I'm not quite sure what to say. I purse my lips whilst nodding and stuff the large bag of medicine into the chest pocket of my leather.

'You know those old rock stars and country singers always rolled around on tour with guns, y'know?'

'I know. It's still a no. But thanks all the same.' I make a turn for the door.

'Well y'know where to find me.' Unfortunately I do, yes.

I lie to everyone. I mean, they know why I'm here. They don't ask questions, but at certain points, they get answers.

We all have our vices. Each and every one of us is a sinner, you're only judged by those sinners who choose to sin differently to you. As a frontman I think I release a certain weight in charisma when I step onto the stage, it differs from night to night, fully dependent on the audience, the venue, the build-up and unfortunately on my own frame of mind and level of intoxication. I know I owe more to my bandmates than I give them on occasion, but I also appreciate that they don't stifle the process that has become a necessity to me. There have been shows that I cannot remember a single second of, I'm not talking about looking back over the years and struggling to pick out one night specifically, but arriving at a bar after a performance or falling onto a hotel bed that very night and asking why we're there already. Why are we in a bar when we have a show to play? Why am I lying on this bed? Aren't we playing soon? *We played the show. Hours ago. Get some fucking sleep.* You think you can ask at that moment, 'how did it go?' But you know better than to pick at that wound. Unfortunately the rolling effect of the shame that I feel the next morning only leads me further towards the desire to drown it out.

Even now, thinking about it, I want to ingest anything that will make me *not*.

Johnny

The long wait between soundcheck and playing. The slow death of time. An ally only to those with a friend to see, a stroll to take or a short nap to be had. It never feels like there's much to explore in your own country, these are the moments made for exotic lands, foreign sights, smells and tastes - a day off under such favourable circumstances can be a gift, but here in the UK a day off feels like a curse or punishment we've been beset with - I can't quite describe just how much I miss touring overseas.

We were on the road when the law was passed and the news channels announced it and the date it was due to come into force was dropped on us like a life sentence. *You no longer have the free right to travel and perform.* We were driving through the Swiss Alps, I can't remember exactly where we had played, maybe Vevey or Martigney, but we were coming down hard, it had been one of those nights. Bad cocaine. We stopped at a service station on receiving the news, it trickled through to each of our phones via different sources, then we all read the official statement together. What we were currently doing was to be outlawed. *Fuck.* And you're standing in this cold drizzly weather, a dam in your nasal passage, staring up at the grand magnitude of these snowy peaked mountains, flanking you on either side, tens of millions of years old, confirming your insignificance as they weigh down on the atmosphere around you. I remember the splintered light reflections disturbing my vision as my eyes grew moist with tears. I think we each suffered our own existential crisis right there on the wet tarmac - which appeared both black and white at the same time - of the high altitude rest stop. I remember Francis buying an ice cream and tearfully lapping at it like a child whilst sitting on a damp rock wrapped up in a huge fur overcoat. It was one of the saddest sights I've ever seen. I steered clear of the extortionate prices of the Swiss service station, I felt worthless enough without opening up my wallet in there.

Holden

Mae and I were sleeping together for a short period some time back, I mean it would hardly constitute a romantic relationship. I love her, she's my best friend, and the sex we shared was intense, raw and animalistic. But it wasn't about that, it was about the comfort, the warmth, the closeness you miss whilst being on the road. Why are we both sleeping in the same room night after night, distantly, in two separate beds? Falling asleep alone. It made no sense. We could be holding each other, sharing a moment, the familiarity of each other's bodies and unique smells. You sleep with such peace, dream with such clarity and wake so much more content when there's someone you love by your side. This entanglement, that is the arrangement as it existed, ended as it was destined to, when a new attraction entered the fold. I had presumed it would be me to lovingly drop Mae when the right after show meet-cute flourished, alas, it was Mae's romance to strike first. And with Isa, I've never bowed out of a love affair with such respect to the incomparable beauty and charm that would replace me.

Mae

Isa approached me after a show in Verona. I was standing at the merch table with Ronnie, I think I signed a record for someone and took a photograph with a couple who held up a t-shirt they had bought. I only remember because that's the moment I saw her, she smiled and stood patiently waiting to talk to me. She held seduction in her employ, like a Helmut Newton photograph. Something fizzled up from deep within. Her eyes didn't leave me. If you traced back their lineage, those eyes have won battles and breached the walls of castles.

'It's so nice to meet you.' She spoke quietly and with a thick Italian accent. I held out my hand and shook hers. Her skin was subtle, dark, silken, animate. Her lips were so full and her eyes so cloudy and dark. I wanted to swim inside of her. No, I wanted to drown.

'You should know,' her voice dropped to a breathy whisper, barely audible over the din of the slowly emptying venue, 'your music, it saved my life.'

'Oh, err... Thank you.' The words never come in reply to a statement like that. I realised I was still holding her hand but I didn't let go, neither did she.

'You should also know,' she paused and pressed her thumb into the back of my hand, 'that sometimes when I masturbate, I listen to your music and I think about you.'

I asked Francis if he minded packing down my equipment and loading the van without me, I wanted to get out of there. He was drunk, he didn't mind. Isa took me to a small nearby bar, a sort of tavern carved out of rock. I paid little to no attention to anything aside from Isa. We drank three or four or five whiskey sours and talked and smoked and when she laughed she stroked my arm and I've never wanted anyone more in my entire life. As Isa talked her left eye would sort of half close whilst the right remained fully open, a kind of involuntary half-wink, it was an adorable imperfection. I wondered whether she noticed any of my flaws and perhaps too found them charming.

After the bar turned us out with the remaining drunks we walked the small streets back to her apartment. We stopped two or three times to make out, she would force me up against the stone of a building that still held the warmth of the day's sun and run her hands through my hair. We didn't sleep that night. We had sex that was healing, erotic, sensual and spiritual. Together, intertwined, you couldn't convince me anything in the world was purer. When morning came I couldn't leave her. I asked, without much hope, if she would join us on the road.

'Where are we going?' She asked. She had just lit her first cigarette of the morning and casually waved away the cloud of smoke that ascended up into her eyes. The tour had five more Italian dates and also a day off in Florence. I told her we would spend every second of the next six days in each other's company. Isa agreed.

We took the back seats of the van and intertwined our bodies like ivy, we fit together naturally like crawling plants with more complex emotions. The rest of the band gave us space, at the time I wasn't alone long enough to discuss what was transpiring with any of them intimately, but they all understood. Holden gave up his bed in our hotel room every night to sleep on the floor in

Francis and Johnny's room, although I think two or three of those he went back to stay with a girl he'd met at the show or the bar afterwards. What a tough time it must have been for *him* in Northern Italy. No, that's unfair, I think he was going through one of his manic low episodes during that period. I remember he was struggling. We'd been sharing a bed and sleeping together for a few weeks before I met Isa. See, Holden and I had sex years before and felt so comfortable that we'd often be naked around each other. That drunkenly opened the way to us sleeping in the same bed and pretty naturally that became sexual, I think I instigated it first, the sex was pretty awful, but then again we were always fairly inebriated, one way or another. Whatever he was going through personally at that time he handled the situation with Isa like a true friend, and I think that period of time was perhaps my favourite within the band. Of course in that moment, playing those shows, watching Isa dance in the crowd every night - honestly that is a form of therapy - and then taking her back to the hotel, in that joy we had no idea the spectre that hung over us. For a mere week and a half after I kissed Isa a tearful goodbye in Milan, vowing that I would return to Verona as soon as the tour was finished, the government implemented the travel ban. Now whilst it is still possible for family, partners and friends to travel abroad to visit those who submit the necessary documentation to allow it, as a touring musician and artist included on what we all ironically - though quite accurately - refer to as the *dissidents list*, it's impossible for me to do so, and neither me nor my closest family or friends can invite Isa here for the same reason. I've simply played one too many protest shows.

So, for now at least, Isa and I are bound to a long distance relationship, very much in love and very much hoping that this period, this climate and its given government, will pass. And as the rain batters the window that my head leans against, as I stare out at the outskirts of Bristol, there's no passing of time, weather or circumstance that I can wait for more than this.

Francis

Holden is a character of both stunning height and quite hopeless gutter wallowing. A paradox I now know I am not alone in seeing. At first it appears oblivious to the others, even if in reality it's not. But his mental trajectory has always looked to be, for me, one aiming towards the pits of Naraka. I've shared some of the heights though, without shame I've rode on those shoulders and supped from his chalice of excess without perhaps concerning myself too much with Holden's personal cost. His almost masochistic decadence. He has this ability to pull you up to his level, he speaks to you just as he sings, with distinguished emotional power. There's a contagious element to that. And you can't escape it, even if you know at times that it's toxic.

When I joined the band, Mae, Johnny and Holden were already close, they seemed to know everything about one another. Shit, I think it was two or three months before I found out that his given name was Stef. Stef Marcus Holden. When we get stopped at a border and the name is read aloud by a strong accent in a uniform, that's one of the only times you see him stripped of something, whether that's the person he is or the character that he's portraying, it's hard to tell. Either way he's my best friend, whether Holden or Stef - and I *will* sometimes laugh - he has my unconditional support. If for no other reason than for the love he has shown me. I know he struggles, he has demons I couldn't think to fend off, but if I'm there, and if I'm able, I'll be fighting them by his side.

Holden

If they knew the darkness inside of me, they wouldn't look at me as though I shine. They romanticise the hedonism, the self-destruction, the addiction, trauma and depression. Should it not be those who claim to care who come to provide the aid? I have my band, but I dare say that's all. Not that I'm ungrateful or searching for more, there are other friends just as close and those who benefit from the business I churn. Maybe I'm being unfair, but it's difficult to wear it on the outside so everyone can see. I feel disconnected, worthless and damaging. My sadness lingers dark and deep, blood coloured. The dank odour of hatred. I've become obsessed. With myself, or with the power I have over others, I'm not entirely sure. It's pure narcissism. Machiavellianism. The dark triad. Inured to this, I now fear the third side. If I'm aware, it can't be true. Can it? Urgh. I should stop mixing drink with these damn pills and get some proper sleep.

Mae

There's something about writing a song, implanting within it that which you didn't know was stored in your mind. Similar to dreaming, your subconscious taps into your hidden emotions and desires. *We all must be who we are.* There are certain idle elements of the self that you simply cannot - or should not - hide from. They can come out more lucid and coherent in a dream than they ever will in the conscious mind. Especially if you're intentionally hiding these truths from yourself. If you're trying to hold on to someone, as you yourself run. If you think that you're binding a person, but in fact are yourself bound. If you're destined to hurt and to hate yourself for it. In my youth I would say that there was nothing I would ever regret, no action or decision, only indecision or the failure to act were to be derided. But now I'm not so sure about that. Now I sense the regret. I feel it. I was writing a song some time ago, clueless to any of this, only to gaze down at the pages and be told by my own consciousness what it knew itself of these dormant thoughts.

I'm sitting at the bar as Johnny soundchecks his drums, *bang, bang, bang,* the monotony of repetition. I raise a freshly prepared gin and tonic to my lips, the cold tiny beads of effervescence jump from the surface of the drink and lightly dance across my face. Whilst working on the beverage, I'm also working on some words. I can hear the melody and I can hear Holden's voice singing. *Bang, bang, bang.*

This evil which we have by birth
This charm inherited by chance

Washed in the artificial light
Spilled down from the ornate antique lamp

I thought I understood your yearning
For it looked identical to mine
I thought I understood your yearning
But you were yearning for another time

Dried flowers hang dead from the gallows
The nails in the walls of your room
Charcoal sketches they lie naked
Across the pages of a novel torn in two

I thought I understood your yearning
For it looked identical to mine
I thought I understood your yearning
But you were yearning for another time

Holden

Mae has set up her laptop backstage and the whole band is sat watching the sinisterly corrupt Great British News - the GBN - broadcast a live stream of Roger Lawrence delivering a statement about the events that have transpired in London over the past two days. He strolls out to the flag drenched podium to address the nation with such a clear lack of emotion it makes me feel nauseous.

To focus on facts - something Lawrence will undoubtedly avoid - in broad daylight and under the gaze of a dozen cameras, two days previously, several police officers beat to death an unarmed, peaceful protester named Marlowe Fonseca. *Beat* to death.

With batons, with boots and with fists. Marlowe had worked closely with a number of organisations aimed at tackling the increasing state surveillance of all British citizens. His aim was to raise awareness, he was a family man, a man of principles, a compassionate human being unsullied by some of the aggression and violence that unfortunately does exist within the anti-government movement. He was a man to look up to, certainly for us, certainly for me. He held a candle of peace, no weapon, no shield to withstand the attack that would steal his life. They claim to have found evidence of plots made by Marlowe to stage protests - peaceful protests - and labelled him a terrorist. It's so convenient for them how this evidence emerges as if from nowhere. As a result the police bludgeoned this man to death in the middle of the street in front of the house where his wife and daughter waited for him to come home. They were unhindered during the attack and remain anonymous as the perpetrators of what can only be classified *legal* by the purest of evil. Roger Lawrence now addresses the nation, not to discuss this, but to condemn the peaceful protest that took place this morning as a reaction to the murder of Marlowe Fonseca. The protesters' crime? They hadn't had the application to protest approved. Now Lawrence stands confidently in front of a camera and declares that *these* people are the criminals.

'Can we turn this shit off?' I ask, but no one acknowledges. I guess they're just too shocked, stunned or absorbed. My words are like stones cast down a long dark well.

I watch myself drag him from his podium, off to the right of the screen and behind the draped flag of this disgraceful monolithic state. Pulling him backwards by the constricting knot of the tie that's closed around his throat of lies, I force him down to the floor as his arms flail helplessly in the oversized suit his frame is unfit to uphold. He lies begging at my feet as I place the sole of my boot over his neck and press down, watching saliva drool from his mouth and his eyes grow bloodshot and desperate as all life ebbs from his wretched body. A grotesque and ugly scene. I shake my head and focus on the laptop screen again. He's still addressing the nation, in that moment condemning the peaceful protest against the police murder of Marlowe Fonseca. *The protesters hadn't had their application for the date approved.* I replay these facts looking for some reason. It was an illegal stand against the seemingly legal slaughter of an innocent citizen. I'm up off the sofa and across the long backstage room, I kick the toilet door wide on its hinges and throw up in the sink. All wine and cold pasta, now having been slightly warmed within my stomach. It just keeps coming up. Mae shouts to ask if I'm ok, but it just keeps coming up.

Francis

It was a difficult show tonight, we were all affected by the topic of death, violence, guilt, innocence and above all the sheer impudence of the PM's speech. Whilst it made me want to play louder and harder and with all that excess zeal and passion, Holden didn't seem himself at all. I know he'd dropped a few more pills than normal before the show, but his performance was in a different place, certainly not on stage with us. His rambling, nonsensical rant about Fonseca's murder was emotionally charged and dedicating the concert to his honour seemed to push the right buttons within the crowd, but he didn't seem fully there with us himself. I must admit I was worried on stage, Mae and I exchanged glances that communicated she felt the same. It was hard work to get through the majority of the set. Holden passed out backstage after the encore and when we came back together to wake him for load-out, we had a small band meeting, hugs and kisses, it all came together and the unit felt whole on leaving the venue. Anyway, London tomorrow, this will be a big show, emotions fully charged, band and audience. You leave behind the negative, there is no revisiting a single moment, no second chance at that show, that look, that conversation, that split second decision, that shot. But we all know that.

Johnny

It's around three in the afternoon, we're about an hour from the venue, just outside of London, on time for soundcheck. The roads are relatively quiet, the weather uncharacteristically nice for that sort of no man's land that lies south of the Watford Gap. In the back of the van we're passing around a bottle of rosé wine that was left over from yesterday's rider, the mood is high. We've come together over what transpired the night before and on the sound system Lee Hazlewood is playing. *Love and Other Crimes.*

We hadn't heard much from Ronnie this tour, traditionally she'd only speak up when we were approaching a border to make sure we were wearing our seatbelts, weren't fucking around or carrying drugs etc. Without again criticising the banality of touring exclusively within the UK, for that reason the occasion for Ronnie to give us a scolding on a border hadn't come up. So when she raises her voice above Lee's raspy baritone and says - 'Guys, we might have a problem.' We turn silent. In that second we all come to our own individual conclusions about what the problem could possibly be, it's unlike Ronnie to raise such concern over nothing, so the looming hurdle we each imagine is substantial in height.

Mae

'A police car is pulling us over.' In that split second I knew that this was no random spot check, Ronnie wouldn't allow a single thing to be out of order with her driving, nor with her van. There's no external reason for them to stop us. They know who we are and they've followed us for this purpose. The heightened interest of those undercover following Holden's lengthy harangue last night. A questionable and unbalanced paranoia shoots through me, but as I glance around at the faces of my bandmates I know this isn't a feeling exclusive to my own mind.

'We're fucked.' Holden says before the final dregs of the bottle of rosé we've been drinking slide down his throat.

'Come on, it'll be fine. We've literally done *nothing* wrong.' Francis has an air of confidence about him that I just don't quite believe. He's right, we hadn't done anything wrong, but that wasn't how this worked anymore.

'We'll see.' Holden utters as he strips out of his leather jacket. 'You know the drill.' We did know the drill, we each shed our leather jackets and began attempting to make the interior of the van look as presentable as possible. By this time Ronnie has pulled us over into an empty gravel lay-by, I draw back the curtain and look out to see that the side of the road lies elevated, a view of fields and woods below, ahead you can see the city clouding the horizon. With the engine shut off I realise just how silent we've all become. I can hear the ringing in my ears from the night before. We sit waiting, I feel for Ronnie being alone in the front but I don't know what helpful support any of our fraught nerves could provide were any of us by her side. Each of our faces holds the same air of concern, etched across our skin like a tattoo declaring our apprehension for what is about to happen.

There are two male officers, they flank us, one on either side. On the driver's side he raps on Ronnie's window and she rolls down to talk, in the back we stay still and quiet in an attempt to make out the conversation taking place in the front.

'Everyone out.' Ronnie turns and tells us, we lock eyes and they betray a concern that I've never seen in her before. We've crossed warzone borders between Russia and Ukraine, argued with and bribed corrupt Moldovan police officers with bottles of cheap French wine, she's wielded a tire iron in the face of a gang of thieves to protect her van, and I've never seen such a look of sincere unease in her before.

Francis slides the door open and we all file out. Ronnie is already standing between the two officers, one looms large and hard like an unforgiving prison guard, the other is shorter and wider and older and for some reason is already holding his baton in his right hand, supporting the end of it in his left. My nerves are shards, slivers of glass. Shivers cut up my spine. Under usual circumstances we would give a greeting, 'afternoon officers.' Or something alike, the silence and the tangible atmosphere, however, speak for the pounding heart in my chest, the sweat from my armpits that runs down my sides and the tremor in my jaw that I attempt to hide by clenching my teeth tight and glancing down at the floor. I notice a scattering of dry, brown and orange leaves, teased across the uneven gravel by a light breeze, are these the earliest of the year to turn crispy and fall?

'I'm not going to entertain the idea that any of you are ignorant enough not to know why we're standing here.' As the taller officer speaks I can feel Holden's riposte welling up from within. My eyes shoot to my right, my head remains still. Telepathically, I beg him not to, obviously to no avail.

'Please, enlighten us.' Oh Holden. The officer steps forward, mountainous.

'What did you say boy? Let me make this profoundly clear, there is no show in London tonight. Your tour is over, so I suggest you get back in your little van and head back to whatever little squat you all reside in.' No one moves, we're frozen in the moment. I want to get back in the van and disappear but I'm terrified to make a gesture for fear it could be misunderstood. I remain motionless, dread and the perception of death, the driving force, the motivation. I can feel my heartbeat pulse throughout every inch of my body and hear nothing above the roaring of blood in my temples.

Holden

The officer towers over me, at around six foot I generally consider myself tall, but this beast of a man dwarfs me. He'd passed beyond a reasonable level of intimidation from the very outset. I attempt to remain calm, strong, reasonable, suppress the insobriety, the desire to scream out.

'Can you explain why this hostility is necessary? What have we actually...' My pacific words are stripped from me as he reaches out and wraps his hand around my throat. Some kind of shocked noise is emitted from every person present, aside from the two in uniform. His fingers dig deep behind my Adam's apple. A stabbing pain fires down my spine.

'You don't speak anymore!' A white froth forms on his lips as he shouts and snarls. Unhinged from any level of decorum he has surely sworn to uphold. The grip tightens before releasing and he turns to Mae, her crying has now become audible over each individual appeal that has died quiet with the growing fear at the burgeoning horror that is the reality of the situation. Francis steps forward and absorbs the focus of both officers.

'Listen, let us just get back in the van. We've done nothing wrong.' His voice is raised slightly in anger or frustration or just in a misplaced bid to try and take back some semblance of control. The shorter, older officer steps forward and raises his baton, Francis cowers backwards as the arm stays aloft above him, the taller officer snorts as his sniggers.

Still smiling he steps forward and places a gloved hand on the side of Mae's head, he steps beside her and runs the hand down her back, she's completely rigid, unable to move, tears stream down her cheeks.

'Don't cry gorgeous.' He murmurs as he continues to run his hand down lower than the base of her spine, she shudders and I jump forward at the same time as Ronnie does. Ronnie is pushed back and struck in the chest by the baton-wielding officer as I bounce off the other in an attempt to push him away. He strikes me hard with a fist to the right side of my face and I see blackness for a split second, on my return to light I am lying in the dirt. I hear the combined shouts of my friends and the officers, I hear Ronnie scream and Johnny bellow out louder than all, I make as much noise as I can until I can make no more.

Mae

The taller officer forces Holden into the ground, the gravel crunches beneath the weight the man places upon my friend. With his knee between Holden's shoulder blades, he forces all air out from within him, he is silenced. What limited breathing he can maintain comes out in spurts of spit bubbles. Francis shouts, instinctively, but all aggression is gone, this is pleading, like that of a child watching a parent be dragged away from them. The shorter, older officer screams in reply, throws his weapon down to the ground and forces Francis against the van, twisting his arm up behind his back in a hold that appears close to wrenching his elbow out from its socket. Everyone's individual screams now build to a cacophony of noise louder and more haunting than the lasting tinnitus our years of touring have scarred us with. It's then that I notice that I've fallen deathly quiet. I close my eyes and seek the dark privacy behind my eyelids. I focus on the feeling of the tears running down my cheeks, one by one, each traces the tracks of the last, fleeing the horrific scene from the point that they gather underneath my chin.

Johnny

Instinctively I pull Mae back and away and she collapses to her knees, I run over to Ronnie who is bleeding from her temple and although staring straight ahead, can't seem to focus. I pick up the baton from the floor and advance towards the officer who has Francis pinned up against the van, it doesn't enter into my mind to actually use the weapon but before this thought is even complete in my mind an enormous weight rushes me from the side and knocks me into the dirt. I take four or maybe five powerful kicks to the ribs and ball myself up in protection against the immense pain. The short, shallow breaths I manage to take between blows weigh pressure on my lungs and my chest tightens in convulsions. Over the pleads and groans coming from all around I hear that the officer is with Mae behind me, but I can't lift myself to turn to open my eyes or hear what is being said. After a moment he shouts to the older officer, who is apparently now finished with silencing Francis, there are no sounds other than Mae's muted weeping and Ronnie's heavy breathing.

'Come on, let's get back. I think they know where they stand now.' I don't catch the inaudible sentence that comes as a reply, but both men let out a disgusting kind of laughter. The only thing that penetrates the seeming calm that now surrounds us is the sound of two sets of boots walking through the kicked up dirt that slowly settles over us. Two car doors slam, the engine starts and the tires spit gravel out over the scene as their yellow and blue battenburg marked vehicle turns out onto the road and we're all swallowed up in a cloud of dust.

Francis

I guess I was momentarily knocked out, I can't remember the strike that did it and the pain in my elbow and shoulder throbs with such severity that it's impossible for me to feel any of the other injuries across my body. I recall everything that happened up until that point, however I have no idea how long I was out for, or what I missed whilst surrounded in darkness and breathing in the tiny rocks and dirt. Holden is lying unconscious beside me, with my good arm I push and roll him over to check that he's still alive, he stirs slightly and comes to. His face smeared with blood and dust, he breathes heavily and coughs uncontrollably. Away, behind the van, Johnny, Mae and Ronnie are sitting amidst the fine, gritty filth in the air that settles around them as they comfort one another. All I can make out over the sharp ringing in the back of my skull is a light sobbing coming from all three. Holden drags himself to a seated position and fixes me with a look of intense pain through heavily bloodshot eyes. We silently share a ventilation of rage and relief.

Part II

Ronnie peels the napkin from the side of her head and examines the dried blood within. 'I'm sorry guys, I have to go home.' There is still a seismic shake in her voice and even with the one arm Francis can still move wrapped around her, she has never looked more alone. We had brought this upon Ronnie and we would all long share the guilt for that.

'Of course, Ronnie. We're all going home.' Johnny says whilst handing her a bottle of water, wincing with a shudder whilst clutching his ribs. Holden hadn't spoken a word yet and I knew what was circling within his mind whilst he sat in the gravel nursing his wounds. He spoke up just as I was thinking it.

'They've beaten us then.'

'Yeah. They've quite literally fucking beaten us.' Johnny's agitated reply comes as he struggles to roll a cigarette, the tremors rattle through his fingers, hands and arms. He throws down the makings and Francis reaches over with a straight cigarette and the flame of a lighter. Each of them cradle an arm or a side or a part of their face that hurts. I'm not quite sure why we're all still sitting in the dirt amidst the site in which this gross abuse had played out. I wonder what the passing cars think has transpired here. Holden coughs deep and heavy, spits up blood and then stands.

'That's it then. We've been silenced.' There *is* a moment of silence before Francis stands up.

'What the *fuck* are you talking about? Look at us. Look at what we've brought upon the people we love. We're lucky to be fucking alive Holden, you realise that, right?' Initially the aggression seems aimed at the air and the situation itself rather than in any personal affront, but Holden was never going to just leave it.

'What did you do Francis? You did fucking nothing. What about Marlowe Fonse...'

'Marlowe Fonseca!? Are you fucking kidding me!? That man was beaten to death in his own street. You don't think he would have rather gone home to his wife and kid that night? That could have been us just now Holden! Any of us! All of us!' Francis lurches forward with the arm he can still move and hits Holden in the chest, the both of them recoil in pain. Under the circumstances, it just appears pathetic. I roll onto my back from my seated position and stare up at the stars that are just beginning to fight their way through the dusk that had unnoticeably crept over and upon us. Francis and Holden continue to fight verbally but my senses have long been blocked to what I can no longer take. Johnny stands and helps Ronnie to her feet.

'Will you be ok to drive or should I?' He asks over the sparring of words that continues to take place in this god awful setting. Whoever's driving, take me away.

'I'll take it easy, but I should be fine.' Ronnie replies, now regaining some of the strength of her natural voice. I stand up myself and Ronnie wraps an arm around my shoulder, she leans her heavy weight against me and presses the sweat soaked strands of her hair against mine, our heads together, she softly tells me that everything is going to be ok, in the same moment Johnny screams at Francis and Holden.

'Guys! Get in the fucking van. We're going

home. It's over.'

Johnny

On getting back into the van the aroma of a previous time emerged and enveloped us, what we once felt and knew would now change. This experience of touring together, if it could ever happen again, would find itself permanently altered.

I sat in the front with Ronnie for the drive back up to Manchester, every now and then I'd ask her if she felt ok, but aside from that we didn't exchange a word. In the back I could hear Mae on numerous phone calls, to Isa, her mum, our booking agent and our label manager, in that order, explaining the story and situation, with slight differences, emphases and omissions, depending on which of the four she was talking to. Other than that the van remained quiet. I'm not sure if Holden and Francis fell asleep or just sat in dead silence. I didn't care, the more time that passed the more my injuries hurt and cradling the left side of my ribs all I could think about was how much worse it could have been.

We each got dropped off at our respective apartments one by one, at each stop we all got out to carefully hug with the intent of shedding the situation of the weight it would undoubtedly hold on our individual relationships. Barely much of any worthy words were exchanged. Holden didn't speak at all. I made arrangements with Ronnie for her to drop the gear at our rehearsal space the following evening, Francis and I would meet her there to unload as it was our *halfway house*, equidistant to where we each lived. To send Ronnie home and spare her that final stretch of the journey, Francis and I decided to walk together, we kissed and hugged Ronnie and she reassured us her husband would look at her injuries as soon as she got home, he's a nurse so she was certainly in better hands than any of the rest of us.

Francis and I walked in silence, dragging our cases, until we hit the crossroads where we part ways. We hugged as long and as strong as our various injuries would allow us.

'Do you think we'll ever play again?' He asked me.

'I guarantee it.' I replied.

'Really?' Francis threw his head back with a light smirk and a chuckle. This was the first time I'd smiled since the light of earlier that afternoon.

'Give it time.' I said and patted Francis on the back as he turned. He grimaced with pain and I raised a blind hand in understanding apology as I too twisted towards my direction.

'I'll see you tomorrow for load-in.' He uttered loudly with his back to me as he crossed the road.

'Load-*out*.' I shouted with my head half turned, home beckoned and I was very nearly there. A short distance from my door I look up at the moon, shrouded in cloud it shines through regardless. One star makes itself known, two, three, four. I consider what we could have done differently to have avoided this outcome and instantly decide that the answer is, 'nothing.' Growing up with my older sister, she had a small poster in her room, tacked to the wall above her desk, adorned with this quote - *We all have one foot in a fairy-tale, and the other in the abyss.* From some corner of my mind it recites itself to me now. I consider my fairy-tale, the good fortune that allowed me to make music for a living, experiencing the best kind of life within this family, this noisy rock and roll band. But the abyss, unfortunately the abyss is this world that we live in.

Holden

The end of this tour, and the band, as I see it, has extinguished something. It was never going to go on forever, such exquisite equilibrium is impossible to maintain. I felt a weight on me to atone, as if it was my sole burden to bear. It wasn't, of course, but I felt myself sinking within a quicksand of my own mixture. *Don't worry my brothers and sisters*, I can take this and more, push forward and move. Move, move, move. Nobody else can feel bad about the thoughts that circle my own mind. In time I will act on them, but for now I will process this trauma in the only way that I know how.

What a terrible handicap it must be to believe you have a soul that will pay the price for the actions you choose to take in life.

Francis

When I got home I drank half a bottle of vodka that I had in the freezer, swallowed a couple of tramadol and slept for about seventeen hours. When I woke I called my mother and then took a taxi to the hospital. I had multiple muscle and bone bruises, a hairline fracture in my radius, damage to the carpal bones, serious twists and sprains within my elbow, and they told me that my shoulder had been dislocated but had since relocated, I can only surmise that it popped back in under the force of the same man who had wrenched it out. Add to that a number of lacerations, one of which on the back of my head required stitches. I got a cast put on my arm and was given a prescription for some heavy duty pain medication. The taxi I took home drove via the pharmacy and the off-licence.

The end of a tour always hits you with a contradictory set of emotions, part relief, part depression. The obscure condition of the mind. There's a sadness that it's over, you'll miss the routine, the travel, playing shows and the general camaraderie. However, it feels good to rest, unload and relax, to have the option of a quiet night in or the luxury of a day in bed. But shit, ending a tour in such a way as this leaves a deep and ugly hole, a hollow emptiness. It feels as though something has been ripped out from within. At the end of a relationship I mourn as if that person has died. I'm afflicted by the same emotion every single time, no matter the duration and even when it's my decision that it must end. It feels deeply unhealthy, but it's self-inflicted in a way, and above all else, in the long term, it will prove to be insignificant. I have the tendency to put my own troubles above those of others, I disassociate myself from the issues of minorities other than those I am familiar with, my own. Where does this come from? The news makes me feel guilty but at the same time powerless to help or make change. I cracked a tasteless joke when it was announced that the homeless and destitute of the country's major cities would be rounded up and placed in *camps-for-work* - it has a really bad taste to it, *work camp*, prisoner-of-war, penal colony, labour camp, internment camp, Gulag - the mind pulls forth the necessary imagery. But my *joke*, I think about that often, and feel a deep sickness upon reflecting on my reaction. Those who protested were in danger of being beaten in the streets, so naturally I didn't join the cause. How many others acted so selfishly? How did it come to this? There used to be an alternative voice, one that spoke reason and was safe to support. Now yet again, like so many, I feel guilty, and so utterly, utterly powerless.

I called Johnny to apologise for not helping load the gear out, making the point that I was currently struggling to lift a cigarette, so shifting a thirty-five kilogram amp down a flight of stairs wasn't looking likely in the near future. The load-in, or out, didn't take place that day. Ronnie required medical attention on returning home - she was now doing fine and being nursed back to full strength by her husband, a man genuinely qualified for that job - Johnny was pretty confident that he had at least one, if not two, broken ribs, but in the knowledge that there's very little a medical professional can do for such an injury, he too took to self-medicating.

We talked about what had happened, to readdress the events helped in acknowledging that this was not some grand figment of our imagination, or a drunken tale exaggerated for effect. No hyperbole would be necessary when recounting this story, and just as it will remain with each of us for the rest of our lives, it was important to address its significance, not just to us personally, but to how it represented the conditions in which we were currently living in this country. I shared my feelings of guilt and the paralysing powerlessness our government has poisoned us with, Johnny shared my sentiment and questioned why we rarely talked about it openly within the band. 'Holden did.' I offered, and we both fell silent. Johnny wouldn't have known through the phone's speaker but I shed a number of silent tears under the weight of the topics we had touched upon. I was, in fairness, incredibly high.

After our throats were cleared and the audible gulps of liquor slowed, we turned to talking about Holden, each expressing our concern about what this might do to his already ragged and fragile mental health. We agreed that we should first deal with our own individual trauma - both mental and physical - before reaching out to bring us all back together, if not as a band, then as a family of best friends. I intended on also calling Mae after I spoke to Johnny, but by the time I had hung up the phone the mixture of pain medication and cheap scotch I had opted for from the off-licence had levelled my basic motor skills. I found myself a mere breath or two from passing out.

Holden

I need to share this hatred, release it upon the world in a manner that any and all can understand. Indisputable, uncompromising violence. The savagery they themselves practice is conveniently veiled from their privileged viewpoint. I wish to fill my fist with the scruff of their neck and force it down into the ground. A badly behaved animal having its face pressed into an excrement and piss soaked carpet. They will know their wrongdoings in having no opportunity to turn away.

In convulsions of sadism I develop my fictitious final act. Daily fantasies in which I imagine the unforgivable beings - primarily the Prime Minister - as the victims of various forms of abduction and torture. Heinous crimes. Not unlike those he has himself committed and sanctioned. At times I question my own seriousness, when modelling my delusional visions on scenes from films that I've seen, or the narratives of books that I've read. In other moments I have not the faintest doubt, not in what my imagination can stretch to, nor in what I myself could be capable of. I feel that this rich tapestry of creations in the back of my mind will later prove to be the precursor to a well-defined plot of seismic proportion.

My fingers hammering away on the keys of my laptop, researching, reading, spiralling, I search for a list of the psychological traits linked to paranoia. That, as an action in itself, should have been included amongst the list. *Pride, anger, excessive rationality, homosexual inclinations, competitiveness, mistrust of emotion, inability to bear criticism, hostile projections and delusions.* I don't really have to stretch my imagination too far to adapt myself to each and every category. A portrait of the paranoid. I'm careful in using my computer and phone, confident as I am that there is still some mild surveillance in place over me. Cooking my brain like this mixture of pills and powders and liquids and dusts that I habitually consume. I need to stock up, provisions, protection and for what may become the means to strike. I can use my phone to contact the Black Country, even if they *are* monitoring, I'm sure they have no qualms with me endangering my health in such a way. And I'm sure even they are unaware as to the nature of my most unreliable friend's newest business venture.

Mae

I thought some isolation might benefit Holden, give him some time and space for self-reflection, perhaps a little internal healing and *shit*, maybe even a period of sobriety. It was a fragile assumption and it would soon crumble under the weight I placed upon it.

There was no contacting him, no phone, message nor email could get through to its target. I visited his apartment every few days, banged on the door and the windows and sat waiting on the staircase in the naïve belief that I'd just missed him on his way out. *Out*, I couldn't imagine where. But there was no sign of life inside. To say this was out of character for Holden would not be entirely accurate. Ever since his mother passed away and he was left without any family, he has been prone to manic-depressive episodes as part of his bipolar disorder, this could include periods of self-imposed seclusion similar to what we're seeing here. I try not to allow my mind to conjure the worst conclusions. I'm confident Holden would never take his own life, not directly at least. The concern comes when you consider how capable the chemicals and concoctions he feeds into his body are at doing this without his consent.

Holden

I'm now live-streaming the GBN all day and all night. I hear the same stories, the propaganda repeated over and over and over again. I'm not sure what kind of sick masochistic pleasure I'm deriving from this, but I cannot seem to turn it off, it's car-crash television, against everything that stirs internally, I cannot look away. Roger Lawrence delivers an announcement every few days that sings untouchable dictator. There appears on the surface a wartime attitude, but the only war that exists is within our own country. How can you rally the troops against their own, against themselves? And to declare that we are in fact *winning*. Against whom and against what? Against *us*? We are rage and hunger, desperately seeking the feeling of being drunk, on the faded colour of poetry and desire, on the present taste of anger and hate. Drink down the richest of wines, try not to focus on the news reports of tormented immigrant families, racism dismissed from the highest rungs of power. We watched it slowly creep in the windows of society, allowing the menace to enter without thinking to shut out the draft and draw the curtains. It moved so quietly at first, but now it shouts, it screams, surely we have more to offer than mere apology.

I turn the volume down and try to read but my focus is simply non-existent. In the bathroom I splash handfuls of cold water up into my face. Assimilating my reflection in the mirror, have I puffed up or drawn skinny and faint? I cannot decide. The dark patches that encircle my eyes, like a sleep deprived raccoon on junk. I regret never really falling in love, at least not to the depths I wish I could have sunk. The opportunity presented itself, though I succumbed to other lustful desires when faced with the chance to stay true and mine deep into what could have been. Had I lived my life with another in such a way, would I now feel regret for the many fleeting encounters and experiences not seized? I very much doubt it, for the unconditional love of one single other is surely what the majority of us would give anything to discover. And in that truth, what possible regret could be felt in finding it.

The many injuries I sustained as a victim of police brutality still remain. The surface evidence of his hands, the cuts and bruises, have all but healed. What remains will never recover. And were I not numbing every cell in my body on a daily basis then my back and chest pain alone would be enough to keep me from sleeping. I have no desire to see or speak to anybody. My sex drive is at absolute zero. My appetite is just about at the level to keep me alive. Whilst my sleeping pattern is inconsistent, the only accordant routine is that I have the urge to throw up almost directly on waking. If I had to describe to a medical professional how I felt, I'd tell them I had *nausea of the cells*. I cut the pills down by almost half - a necessary cull due to the quantity remaining - and try to curb the drinking, but I fall so low I need something to pull me up and so I arrange a drop off of Amphetamine reinforcements. This does something for my focus but very little for my appetite. I've put off the journey down to the Midlands for the past few days, as physically incapable as I have been of executing it. But tomorrow a small number of trains are all that stand between me sitting back here, fully stocked and wielding, for the sake of what is left to love about this country, a - possibly defective - handgun.

Francis

I take a call from Mae and she asks if I've heard from Holden. 'If you haven't, then I haven't.' I told her. Holden cares more about Mae than any other person, it'll be her phone that lights up first when he's ready to reach out. She's worried, I mean I understand, but I know Holden and I know he's holed up in his flat drinking hard and snorting or swallowing whatever he's choosing to numb what's circling within his head. It's a concern, obviously, but I'm also trying to bring myself back to a reality that I want to live in. I'm not a young man anymore, I can't swim this darkness. I'm alone and I'm going to try, but I have to focus on the individual. I love Holden. I love Mae. I love Johnny. I just don't know what I can do for my brothers and sister at this time.

Holden

The train voyage to the Black Country, despite a cancellation, a delay and at least one change more than is necessary for the journey, went as smooth as could be expected. I had a valid ticket and kept myself from falling asleep and missing a stop by indulging in semi-regular bumps of speed, courtesy of the deal for a deal package that I was delivering to my untrustworthy business partner for a discounted cost on what I would be bringing back with me.

Arriving at Tipton I was so wired that my thoughts were as sharp as a dart point and I took a taxi straight to the flat and asked the driver to wait outside and keep the meter running. There was so much speed-riddled focus and conversation regarding the uppers for downers deal we were undertaking, that the gun was essentially tossed like a bonus gift into the top of my bag mere moments before I left the door. The prize at the bottom of a cereal box. I didn't think to ask how it works, if it was loaded or indeed how I would even go about doing such a thing. Questions like, *what kind of licensing do I claim that I have if I am caught in possession*, couldn't have been further from my mind. I mean, I'm quietly confident not a single person in that flat would have had the first clue to the answer to any of those questions themselves, but I was sat in the back of the taxi and en route back to the train station before I even considered what I *should* have asked and what *should* have been at the forefront of my mind. Curse the myth of amphetamine fluency.

Back at the station awaiting the connection up to Wolverhampton, I caught sight of the destinations the train heading in the opposite direction was destined for. My mother was born, raised, lived and died in Astwood Bank, a forty-five minute drive south of where I now found myself, for reasons I never could have dreamt explaining to her.

She raised me alone, following my father's death at the behest of a machine I am told he knew and manned with more experience and knowledge than anyone else in the factory he worked. Basic negligence led him to try and fix a faulty cog system without shutting down the power and when it fired up and took half of his arm into the interior mechanism he passed out from the shock. He died in the ambulance on the way to the hospital. My mother always claimed that his life could have been saved by a faster response team, but how much blame can you place on another person or an institution - the health service I was born into but will now, thanks to this government, die without - for a situation such as that.

I don't remember a single thing about him. My knowledge of how he looked comes solely from photographs. Regardless of the tragedy, my mother raised me well. I guess the focus on me and my upbringing kept the grief from consuming her. She never remarried and any man who attempted to enter our life was either driven away by the part of the petulant child that I played, or the fact that he was quite simply never going to be the man my mother loved and mourned for every day of her life. We were inseparably close as I grew up, I would discuss each and every angle of my school life, and as I matured, no topic was beyond reasonable conversation. Relationships, sex, career ideas, any and all aspects of the future.

I left a part of my heart behind with her when I left for Manchester to start university. It was during my first or second year there that I sought the escapism of drink and drugs to numb how I felt about what I saw internally as leaving my mother and her solitude behind me. She was supportive until the very end and whilst she knew that I would never return home, I always maintained that one day I would. Of course, and inevitably, I never did, and shortly before finishing that redundant degree I met Mae and Johnny and we started the band. We lived wild and cheap and my contact with my mother withdrew from daily phone calls to those only accepted weekly. Certain girls I would be seeing would curse her name when it illuminated my phone screen, I wouldn't answer for that reason, and I fucking hate myself for that. I would visit home more when the opportunity suited me, rather than when I was able. And when I found out she was ill I was tripping on acid and hadn't slept for three days, so I waited another two before travelling down to be with her. We had a tour booked, Mae told me that we could and should cancel it, but my mother was back at home and feeling better and she told me to do it. 'Go on tour. Go and do it.' She repeated. Her exact continuous phrase, like a lightning bolt shooting down in the middle of our otherwise unrelated conversations. All I could say to fall on deaf ears was, 'no.' She told me she'd still be waiting in bed to be taken care of as soon as I got back. And eventually, with her trademark stubborn effort, she persuaded me. I told her that I'd bring back some of those creamy Belgian chocolates that she loved so much. And I left. I'll never forget the honesty and what I like to perceive as pride in the smile she gave me as I left.

We walked off stage in Hamburg and I hugged the band and sunk into a sofa and lit a cigarette and took the phone from my jacket and I saw the missed calls and I knew what news they were attempting to deliver to me. My mother had died whilst I was on stage, feigning emotions and singing words Mae had written to lost lovers. My mother had died and I could have been by her side, for that last word, that last look, to hold her hand and tell her just how much I loved her. But I was sitting in the stinking backstage of an overcrowded venue, watching my bandmates and some people I didn't even know spill drinks all over each other. I think it took them some time before they realised why I was crying. Mae fell down on me first, she knew I shouldn't have been there. I *should* have been telling my mother just how much I loved her.

I feel a tear roll down my cheek and realise it's not the first. I've just been standing here leaking tears onto the train platform, absent but for the memories that replayed behind my eyes. The tannoy system announces the train's arrival and I turn to see it approaching. Jesus, the speed has well and truly worn off, all this emotion wrenching me up and out from within. Don't think about it right now. Sit down, swallow a pill and get back home.

Johnny

'I'm not a philistine.' Holden once assured me as we sat outside a restaurant in Thessaloniki. I'd asked him why he hadn't started eating after the waiter had delivered our dishes and the rest of us were already deep in the process of enjoying our food. He was waiting for a glass of wine before he started eating. There is a beauty to that stubbornness that was characteristic of everything that Holden did. It was in that personality trait that I found the explanation for why he hadn't answered any of our calls over the past weeks. I'd visited the apartment with Mae and we'd given the door a beating and waited around outside for a while before giving up and heading to the pub for a drink. I'm sure there was more that we could do, but as we discussed it over a few pints, we couldn't define exactly what that would entail. Aside from knocking down the door and forcing entry, we drew complete blanks. He needed, or at least wanted, solitude, and even in the understanding that that isn't the best for this person, you can't force yourself upon them, just as you can't force yourself through that locked door. When it did open, we would be there, but for now all we could do was wait outside, or in the warmth and shelter of the nearest pub. After all, we're not philistines.

Holden

I was being lured to death as a constant topic. Death. Revenge. These heinous acts of terrorism swam through my consciousness like those of a sexual nature do a nymphomaniac. I'd never fired a gun before, never held one before this. The unexpected weight made it feel important, it carried the gravity of what it was capable of. But was I? In heart I held a twisted belief, but in action I was inexperienced, worse, I was a coward. I question the intelligence and sanity of the perpetrators of such acts, yet how absurd as I now stand questioning myself.

I spend hours reading. Time is moving so slowly. I feel tired, antiquated. I begin writing long twisted letters to no one in particular, I write to the alive and to the dead, my father, my mother amongst them. Old lovers, the girls and boys of aftershow hotel rooms, even those whose names I hadn't the faintest memory of. I knew not what to take from this internal council, this constant scrawling, it continued regardless. It didn't frighten me, nothing I could think up or do could frighten me anymore.

I decided to write a letter to him, *Dear Mr Prime Minister*. I write that the spectre of death is lingering. The night of the assassins is upon us. I enclose my own illustration of his obituary, it reads like that of a disgraced tyrant, one that I hope is lost to the annals of history. Forgotten or cursed as a nation's regret. I spit on the scrawled letter and rip it up into shreds on the desk before me.

I'm tired. I'm tired with the weight which I never asked to bear. When did I last sleep? When did I last eat? Now that I focussed on the thought I realised my stomach was contracting and aching with hunger. It made me retch, nothing but a splash of pale bile came up, it lay on the surface of the carpet before slowly soaking in, the sight of which made me retch again. I felt a nausea bubbling up from deep inside of me. I left the desk and its surrounding area in the state of disarray it had degenerated to over the past weeks and climbed into bed, somewhere between the sickness and the throbbing my eyes closed, and I managed to fall asleep.

On waking I hear a reporter on the GBN - I've become so familiar with the voices of the individual correspondents that I can tell without looking that it's Jennifer Greene - Sir Roger Lawrence will deliver a leader's speech to the public on the South Bank of Westminster Bridge a week from today. Propped up on the sofa, a stale taste of vomit in my mouth, I rely on my laptop to ask the necessary questions of the official party website and receive back the answers I had hoped for. No tickets or reservations are required to attend or enter the event. It's merely a case of being there early enough and eagerly queuing that will secure you a shot at being a stone's throw away from the Prime Minister.

Mae

I created this band, I brought the members together and drove it from pipe dream to reality. With Johnny I christened it with a name and with the songs I wrote and the words I gave to Holden, I helped him discover his voice. Each and every one of them carved out a corner of the band for themselves and found in it whatever it was that fulfilled them. Vice's aside, it was first and foremost about the music, for *all* of us. We've travelled the world and experienced so much together. Blood aside, we're more than family.

To be thrust into an assessment upon the experience of being in a band, on a base level, you would analyse the live performance, the dizzying carnival that is the hour or two you spend on stage each night. The noise, the interaction, the feeding off one another, a starvation that can only be quelled by those in your select group. The ability to predict what is coming next and where it will go from there, whether rehearsed or not, a maze made by one can be navigated by all. But just as a human body, absolutely none of that surface exists without the gruesome innards that strain and pump away to lead it all to work. That's what being in a touring band is, you live through the blood and the guts and the viscera and the filth, all for that short moment every day during which you can step outside and appreciate what that internal mechanism has created. And it's the time spent in the innards, the rehearsals, the van, the hotels, the bars, the backstages, that makes it all work when it comes to the surface. And when the insides are healthy and it all works as one, then there's no feeling better than when you make that step out. I wouldn't want to be part of an unhealthy anatomy, a noxious, diseased, sickly organism.

I miss the body we shared as The Collectors. I miss the road, I miss the stage, I miss Ronnie and I miss my brothers.

Holden

It's difficult to ignore your best friend banging on your door every few days, but whilst I don't have any intention to answer, it feels better than any of the other highs or lows that I'm relying on, just to know that any kind of care exists. It's been going on for weeks now, which reinforces the reasoning, the feeling, that I can't bring myself to reach out. My own pride has eroded to nothing under the waves of the - admittedly short - period of time that has passed in such regrettable ignorance. Anyway, regardless of that and much else, I probably should focus, my decision has been made, my destination, my pursuit. Tomorrow I will travel to London.

I book a room in a familiar ambiguous hotel in Elephant and Castle, a short walk from the bridge, although in an understandably over the top state of paranoia, I will stick within crowds and most likely ride the Underground the short distance up to Waterloo. That way I can stay curtained and concealed within the droves of supporters that I will undoubtedly be battling with for a spot once I arrive there. I will paint on the face of excitement and awe in a bid to disguise that which I truly wear, the face of the amateur executioner.

The bag I pack is minimal, suiting my intended destination. As opposed to my journey down to the Midlands, that which delivers me to London is a single, straightforward and, by comparison, luxury train. The prospect of tomorrow weighs heavily on me, as do the thoughts of loose ends left dangling. But my focus must be, and will remain, that of the grand oration.

On arriving at Euston station I catch the Northern line down to Elephant and Castle, check in to the hotel and leave my bag, before visiting one of my favoured local pubs for one last civilised pint. There are not many establishments left standing that can do justice to the ten guidelines for the ideal public house, as declared by George Orwell in his essay *The Moon Under Water*, but this place ticks a couple of boxes, and if this is to be where I should sup my final drink in such a fashion, then what better a place.

The comfort of the barstool that supports me does its bitter best to share the weight that presses down upon my shoulders. My elbows resting on the bar, I stare down between my legs at the carpet of civilised burgundy red, absorber of more liquids than I. No music plays, only the low murmuring voices of the older pub men create the atmosphere. Waves of realisation crash against me, threatening to topple me back off of my stool. I revert from man to child, all sense of myself as an adult feels momentarily distant. I am penetrated deep inside by a riddle that

I fear I will never solve. I imagine when someone considers an act, the like of which I am currently, they shouldn't feel dead inside, there should be a war within the self. My own war was waged some time before and the battles have long since been raging, though I feel now, here, a surrender is taking place. A victory. The loser concedes and must expiate the time spent in opposition. The queen long gone, the king marooned, soon to be expired. Checkmate. Johnny and I would play chess in the back of the van, of countless games I beat him only once. The unanticipated victory is the one you cling to, the one remembered above all other notches. Even after the war is over, the treaties signed and the withdrawal complete, there are the hideous ugly tasks that remain, those that must be completed, cleaned up, like mine tomorrow.

That one final drink turned into four pints and a few shorts but I'm back up in the hotel room and in bed early enough to make the alarm for the next morning. I'm not on tour, this is one wakeup call I will not get, and no one is going to be waiting for me.

With personal surprise I awake before the sound of my alarm has chance to chime, the early morning sun glares heavy through the window, the curtains of which I didn't think to draw last night. I take a long and very hot shower, not washing or scrubbing at my body, but just standing still beneath the cascading water. I consider the focus, that which I thought I would lack, but which is currently pulsing through me with vehemence. I dress in the single set of clothes that I have with me and sit on the end of the bed to examine the handgun on which almost all responsibility now lies. The image frightens me,

I stuff it deep into the right hand pocket of my long overcoat and leave the room, leave the hotel, and walk to the Underground station.

With every step I expect to feel the weight of authority come down as a hand on my shoulder. Now standing cold, yet perspiring pure heated venom on a crowded train, I ask myself - are we really not better protected than this? Is their surveillance all but an illusion? How did I slip through the net and swim this far, so close as I now am to the heart. Is the state merely feigning control when in fact they have none? Is the affectation of what they are capable of existing simply to disguise the façade? I have no answers to these questions, and I must remind myself that my purpose here is not to find out. I have a task to complete and I'm getting oh so very close. Their threats are empty, nothingness, action is the only thing tangible. My very own action, which has until this point, escaped them. The train pulls into Waterloo and pretty much the entire population of passengers exit to file out and up towards the site at which Sir Roger Lawrence will give his speech in a few hours time.

My stomach convulses and halts my ability to walk for a beat. I pass through a tunnel unlike the system of the underground train, a black out, before a collection of lanterns appear dangling from side to side, bejewelled with colour and light. In this deep grotto I feel stripped, naked and vulnerable. No panic overcomes me, but a grave has opened up within, deep in the bottom of my bowels. Stabbed in the gut by a rapacious desire to drink, I straighten and absorb my surroundings on the Underground platform. Riding the rapids of an internal sickness, sloshing from one side to the other. Balance a long lost and forgotten art form, I attempt to steady myself. No doubt a small glass of something would help, but I fully understand that the price of stepping into a pub for that leveller, would mean only the complete failure of the duty I have come here to fulfil.

I focus on any hands in pockets like my own, there's so many of them. Who else has their cold hand upon a weapon and who is *their* target? Me? Do we share the same prey? If so I leave this job to you. So much more competent you undoubtedly are. Take this weight from my pocket, from my hand, from my mind. I'm surrounded by his jubilant supporters, the garrulous masses, children waving flags. Who are these people who support what this country has become? Who would allow their child to idolise a monster?

I feel the weight of the gun in my pocket. I can feel my heartbeat in the thumb I press into the raised dimples that adorn the grip. I know nothing about this machine of death that I hold so tight. I've done nothing to earn this right, this power over life and death that it gives me. I didn't even load the magazine myself, I had to search online how to remove the lock, how to pull back the slide. I've not practiced a single shot. I have no idea what it feels like. No, I leave that to the prurient ballistic experts. Since I'm out here on my own. If this doesn't work then it has been for nothing, but what more do I have left to give?

CCTV cameras loom heavily over me, crouched atop doorways, gates and entrances, unblinking but somehow unaware. I'm essentially corralled all the way from the station to the site where the speech will take place, though I am astounded by the sheer lack of supporters, such a vast contrast to what I was expecting to be faced with. Looking around at the reality of this event, the prospective numbers the GBN boasted have been slashed by considerably more than half. Maybe even less. Though no *reality* will be reported here today, regardless of the outcome. This is the age of delivering a speech to one man and telling everyone who wasn't there that you spoke to thousands. For me, anyway, it works in a fine way to my favour.

It takes some time to squeeze through certain groups, simulating the action of waving to an imaginary someone closer to the front and then passing through to *join* them. I have flashbacks to doing the same at many crowded concerts in the past, a pang of nostalgia hits me, for what I have been lucky to experience, and for what I never will again. I keep moving forward. Before long I am in position about five or six rows from the front and slightly off to the right of the stage, it would be impossible to get closer but I settle and am comfortable in the space. Whilst the police gather heavily in attendance, they act only as the walls of a barricade around us as opposed to walking amidst, I feel safely camouflaged where I stand. Insignificant and unnoticeable, a blend of all that surrounds me, the antithesis of all that I have ever aimed for as an artist. The great difficulty of this moment is to integrate amongst these people, to witness and appreciate them as fellow human beings, but to hear their conversations, their opinions, their beliefs and their misplaced pride and support for what will shortly be paraded across the stage before us.

As time passes I become concerned as the

crowd grows somewhat steadily and we're cramped more sardine-like towards the front. I gain some ground but lose the freedom of space and movement around me. He's running behind his scheduled time of appearance. I momentarily worry that he's been tipped off, that all along they *were* on to me and I've been lured into a trap. No. No, then I think about the amount of times we too as a band have pulled this act. Delaying your appearance on stage to build anticipation. He's a performer. As I dwell on the one thing I've found that we have in common, he walks out on stage to the thunderous applause of those around me. The parallel suddenly hits me harder, harder than that officer drove me into the dust, his acclamation, his act, his stage is not too dissimilar to that which I have forever craved. Are we in some way kindred? Assimilating, I too give a light clap not to seem out of place, taking my hand from the grip of the gun for the first time since leaving the hotel, I realise just how clammy with sweat it has become. I wipe the hand down my thigh and replace it deep into the pocket where it belongs. As the noise subsides Lawrence smiles and raises his arms before bellowing a greeting into the microphone and launching into his pre-prepared speech.

I waited patiently for my moment, nerves wracked but somehow lucidly calm. I don't focus on the words he speaks out as I know they will only further rile me and disturb the clarity I will very soon need. I glance to my left at a young man, his face wrought with a saddened look of vulnerability, a look that has been disregarded so many times before that he is searching here for an answer, for a meaning, for a purpose, all in vain. The crowd settles and sinks into an air of passivity as Roger Lawrence talks, occasionally when baited they give a moronic roar, a braindead cheer. I go through the motions, thinking *now*, no *now*, no. *Now*. I run the back of my free hand across my forehead and make my move. Now.

I push the man in front to clear a path and pull out the hand that holds the weapon tightly through a layer of sweat. I aim it at Sir Roger Lawrence's chest and close my grip, the trigger is harder to pull than I imagined but it clicks, shudders, a shot rings out and the recoil pushes my arm up, back and to the right. Everything goes momentarily silent before erupting with noise. I pull my arm back down and aim for a second shot, I feel everything closing in, bodies move away as others grow closer, amidst overwhelming noise and chaos my second shot rings out, as does another from elsewhere, an ignited fire hits me, my neck jerks as I fall, tackled, I'm accompanied to the ground, the burning sensation shoots up my spine and then darkness finally falls.

Heavier Than a Death in the Family

Johnny

I remember when Mae and I decided to call the band The Night Collectors. We were young, sitting in her bedroom, listening to records, drinking beer and smoking stolen cigarettes. Shit, I really had a crush on her back then, it would have seemed inconceivable to me at that point that we would end up being something of a brother and sister. Well, it's *inconceivable* that it all came to an end like this. Anyway, The Night Collectors, it's the title of the second track from Les Rallizes Dénudés' live record *Heavier Than a Death in the Family*. Ironically the track that follows it is titled Night of the Assassins. *Night of the fucking Assassins.*

Of all the ugly events that followed what happened, the only thing we tried to focus upon was our memory of Holden, the person we knew, loved and cared for. Everything was going to change, but we couldn't be certain of anything except for the fact that that's exactly what he would have wanted. Perhaps we never spoke enough about what Holden had to offer music as an artform, but it was precisely what he stood so passionately for in life, an unconditional form of freedom.

He had left one lone hand scrawled note on the desk in his flat, and it read -

Mae, Johnny and Francis. I love you all. Do not mourn, celebrate, for I bid farewell to the illness that is consciousness. In honesty, I now find reality an absolute and indefinable terror. Eroding away as

*it crashes against me, I choose to give in to the current
and drown myself rather than stand the beating of
the breakers. Farewell.*

Here's to you Holden.

ALSO OUT ON FAR WEST

farwestpress.com

+1 (541) FAR-WEST

www.ingramcontent.com/pod-product-compliance
Lightning Source LLC
Chambersburg PA
CBHW020049310726
48970CB00007B/2484